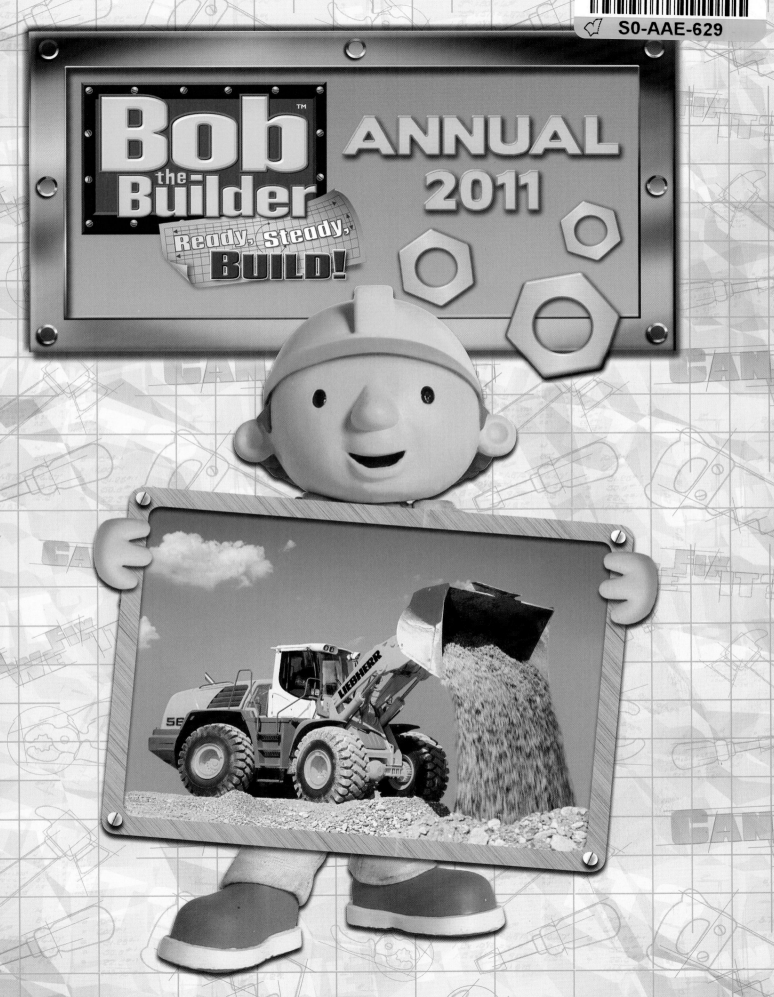

Bob the Builder

the

Ready, steady, BUILD!

ANNUAL 2011

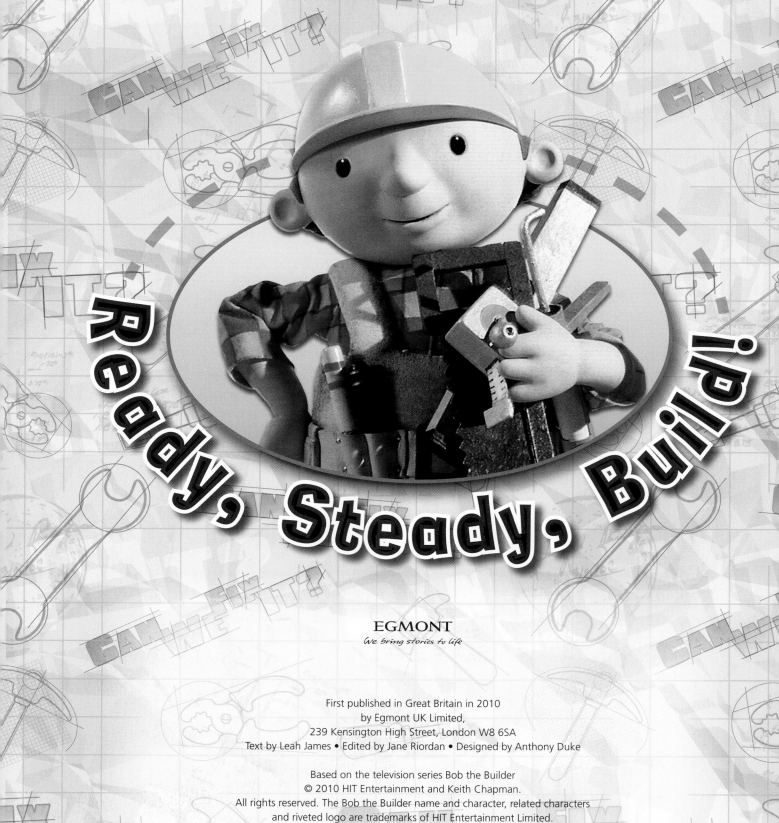

Ready, Steady, Build!

EGMONT
We bring stories to life

First published in Great Britain in 2010
by Egmont UK Limited,
239 Kensington High Street, London W8 6SA
Text by Leah James • Edited by Jane Riordan • Designed by Anthony Duke

Based on the television series Bob the Builder
© 2010 HIT Entertainment and Keith Chapman.
All rights reserved. The Bob the Builder name and character, related characters
and riveted logo are trademarks of HIT Entertainment Limited.
Additional images by kind permission of Daf Trucks Ltd, Liebherr, Renault Trucks and Scania Image Desk.

ISBN 978 1 4052 5251 5
1 3 5 7 9 10 8 6 4 2
Printed in Italy

Contents

The Machine Team

I'm the orange cement mixer, Dizzy.
I love to giggle and chatter and
I'm always full of questions.
Brilliant!

Muck by name and
Muck by nature.
I always get my red
paintwork mucky! I can
dig and move heavy loads
but just don't ask me
to work at night –
I'm afraid of the dark!

It's Scrambler here. I'm a blue,
all-terrain, four-wheel drive vehicle.
Check me out when I go
off-roading. Wicked!
Sunflower Valley rocks!

I'm Lofty, a tall, blue, mobile crane. One of my favourite tools is my demolition ball. I get a little worried about working on big jobs but I can do it – **er, well I think so.**

You probably know me, I'm Scoop, the yellow digger. I'm always full of big ideas. I love to get the job done but always have time for a joke along the way! **No prob, Bob.**

Hi there, I'm Roley the green steamroller who loves to sing! If Bob needs a road smoothed or dirt flattened, I'll be there. **Let's rock and roll!**

And last but not least, I'm Benny – Speedy Benny. I'm a digger like Scoop, I just wish I was as big as him. Check out my bright pink paintwork. **Unreal Banana Peel!**

Meet The REAL Machines

It's Bob the Builder here. Say hello to a whole new machine team, the REAL machines. They are big and strong and ready for work!

cab

drum

ladder

concrete truck mixer

loader

bucket

boom

steps

tyre

bucket

tracks

excavator

open-box bed

mirrors

dumper truck

hook

cab

boom

truck

jack

truck-mounted crane

11

Radio Bob

"**Hello, Flex!**" said Wendy, one morning. Flex was giving Bob a lift in his basket. He was looking at a plant while he waited.

"**Do you know a lot about plants?**" Wendy asked.

"**Er, oh, I do, Wendy! This one's a Many-Coloured Mountain Creeper.**"

"**Wow!**" smiled Wendy.

"**But don't tell anyone!**" said Flex. "**It's not very interesting, is it?**"

Before Wendy could reply, Bob had finished and they went back to the team.

Bob and Wendy showed the team plans for a new Sunflower Valley radio station and mast. Mr Bentley was in charge of the radio shows. Each machine had to think of one idea for their very own show!

"**OK, team,**" said Bob. "**Can we build it?**"

"**Yes, we can!**"

Bob jumped on to Scoop. "**Flex, could you give me a lift later?**"

"**OK, Bob!**" said Flex as he trundled off to think of an exciting idea.

At Scarecrow Cottage, Farmer Pickles was tuning his radio. Flex was watching Scruffty play nearby, when he noticed a plant.

"It's a rare Blue-Striped Hill Fern!" Flex said to Scruffty.

Scruffty panted and ran off to play.

"Never mind, Scruffty," sighed Flex. **"It's not very interesting …"**

Suddenly, the radio blared out, **"The coolest show there's ever been, Radio Seventeen!"**

"What's that?" asked Flex.

"That's a radio jingle!" said Farmer Pickles.

"A jingle, what an exciting idea!" thought Flex.

… **Radio Seventeen!**

When Flex arrived back at the build, Roley, Dizzy and Dodger were singing to Mr Bentley,

"Doo, be doo, be doo, be doo, a radio station … just for you!"

"A jingle! They've already thought of my idea." Flex sighed. **"Mr Bentley, can you help me have an idea, please?"**

"Ah, well, how about telling jokes?"

"Hmmm," thought Flex, **"that's a good idea."**

Later that afternoon, the machine team gathered around Dodger.

"**What happened when the steamroller drove over a duck's egg?**" asked Dodger.

"**I don't know, Dodger!**" said Dizzy.

"**He … quacked it! Quack, quack!**"

"**I'll never tell jokes as well as Dodger!**" thought Flex. He wandered off, thinking.

"**Don't forget I'm going to need a lift later, Flex!**" Bob called after him.

Flex wandered on until he saw a pile of pineapples by Mr Beasley's yurt.

"**Mr Beasley, this pineapple's a rare species!**" said Flex. "**The Peruvian Spiny!**"

Mr Beasley looked confused.

"**Oh, don't worry, it's not very interesting … Have you got any ideas for a radio show?**"

"**How about story time?**" suggested Mr Beasley.

"**Great idea!**" said Flex.

Quack, quack!

Back on site, Lofty and Scoop put together the studio while Packer helped Bob and Wendy to unpack the speakers.

When Flex arrived, Lofty, Scoop and Muck were gathered around a microphone.

"Hello, and welcome to Muck and Scoop's Story Time!" practised Lofty.

"Oh no!" panicked Flex. **"Story time was my idea!"**

Lofty and Bob lifted the final section of the mast into place.

"Now, let's fix the transmitter to the top!" said Bob. **"Ready, Flex?"**

But Flex had gone!

"If we haven't got Flex to fix the transmitter," said Scoop, **"we can't broadcast Bob FM!"**

Bob, Scoop and Dizzy went off to find Flex. He was with Farmer Pickles and Mr Beasley, trying to tune in to Bob FM.

"Flex! Bob FM needs you!" cried Scoop.

"No it doesn't, I haven't had one idea for an exciting show," replied Flex.

"Not for a show, Flex. To give Bob a lift to fix the transmitter!" said Dizzy.

"What happened, Flex?" asked Wendy, riding in on Roley.

"I forgot to help Bob!" worried Flex. **"I was busy trying to think up an exciting show for the radio!"**

Wendy spotted a plant nearby. **"Isn't that the same plant you showed me earlier?"**

"Yes, but ..."

"Well, why don't you do a show about plants?"

"Because it's not very interesting," said Flex.

"Yes it is!" said the team.

Everyone hurried back to the station, where Flex and Bob fixed the transmitter to the mast. Bob FM was ready to go!

After Muck and Scoop's Story Time finished, Flex's Plant Watch began. Flex told everyone about the amazing plants Bob could see through his binoculars.

"Plant Watch is really exciting, isn't it?" Dizzy said to Mr Bentley.

"Yes, Dizzy," Mr Bentley replied. **"Flex did have an exciting idea, after all!"**

Welcome to Plant Watch!

Odd One Out

One of these pictures of fantastic Flex is missing something.
Can you tell which one it is, and what is missing?

Answer on page 68.

Cherry Picker Close-ups

These four close-ups can all be found in the big picture.
Circle them when you have found them.

Cherry pickers have an amazing flexible
arm and a basket. They lift people up high!

Scrambler Gets Prepared

One afternoon in Sunflower Valley, Bob and the team were building a log cabin.

"What's it for, Bob?" asked Scrambler.

"It's for guests to stay in when they're exploring the forests and mountains," replied Bob. "And the first guests, Badger Patrol, are coming tonight."

Sunny, Saffron, Cassia and Carlo were at the dome with Chip Chipper, the leader of Badger Patrol.

"Right," said Chip. "Tonight, we'll see some badgers."

"Hoorah!" cheered the children as Scrambler zoomed up.

"Right on time, Scrambler," said Chip. "You're in Badger Patrol today!"

"Wicked!" said Scrambler. "What do I do?"

"Just follow our motto, and 'Be prepared'!" said Chip.

Scrambler went to find Roley to ask about being prepared.

"Roley, what do people in the woods need the most?"

"Shelter is important, in case the weather is bad," Roley replied.

"Thanks, Roley!" Scrambler whizzed off to take the children into the woods.

At the campsite, Chip wanted to tell Scrambler something, but Scrambler was in a hurry!

"Sorry, Chip, I have to go. I need to be prepared!"

"But I want to tell you about the shelter …" called Chip. But Scrambler didn't hear.

21

Mrs Bentley was closing up the General Store when Scrambler arrived.

"I need a tent, please!" cried Scrambler.

Mrs Bentley fetched a tent and placed it in Scrambler's trailer. Scrambler zoomed back to see Roley.

"Is shelter all I need?" he asked.

"And food," said Roley. **"That's the other important thing."**

"Oh no!" Scrambler raced off to the campsite, just as Lofty and Roley pushed the last log of the cabin into place.

"I've brought shelter!" cried Scrambler, pulling into the campsite.

"We're building our own shelter, out of things we found in the woods," said Chip. **"It's called a bivouac. I did try to tell you …"**

"Oh no, I wasn't prepared! I'll go and get the other thing we need!" And off Scrambler went again, without hearing Chip call, **"But Scrambler, we're already prepared!"**

Scrambler found Mrs Bentley on her way home. They went back to the store and put some fruit, sunflower seeds and nuts into Scrambler's trailer. He scrammed back to Roley.

"Shelter and food are all I need, right?" asked Scrambler.

"Yep!" said Roley. "Oh and warmth. Shelter, food and warmth are the three most important things."

"Oh no! Three things?" Scrambler rumbled off as Lofty lowered the log cabin's roof into place.

"I'm prepared, I've brought food!" said Scrambler, roaring into the campsite.

We've already got energy bars!

said Chip with his mouth full.

"Oh no. I've only got one more chance to be prepared!" Scrambler rushed off and screeched to a halt outside Mr and Mrs Bentley's hill-house.

"Mrs Bentley!" he called. "Help! Badger Patrol needs warmth!"

Still wearing her nightdress, Mrs Bentley climbed on to Scrambler. At the store, she found some jumpers and packed them into Scrambler's trailer.

Bob and his team were admiring the finished cabin, when Scrambler pulled up.

"**Good timing, Scrambler!**" said Bob. "**It's time to pick up the children.**"

"**But I haven't taken their jumpers yet!**" said Scrambler. He raced off, with Bob and Roley following.

In the woods, the Badger Patrol was gathered around a hole.

"**This is a badger's burrow, called a sett,**" whispered Chip. "**Be really quiet!**"

A snuffling snout came out of the hole just as Scrambler came tearing in,

"**I've got warm clothing, I'm prepared!**"

The badger disappeared back into the burrow.

"**Scrambler, you've scared the badger away!**" said Chip.

Scrambler stopped. "**But I thought you needed warmth?**"

"**We've got Badger Patrol jackets,**" Saffron said.

"**Oh no, I've messed up. I wish I could make the badger come back,**" said Scrambler.

"**You could use nuts and seeds to bring him out,**" suggested Roley.

"**Wicked, that's exactly the food I've got! I'm prepared!**" said Scrambler.

Later that night, Chip laid a long line of fruit, seeds and nuts around the sett. Everyone waited quietly as a badger came out, followed by some baby badgers. They ate the food and went back inside.

"**Well done, you were prepared!**" said Chip.
He stuck a Badger Patrol sticker on to Scrambler.

"**Wicked!**" said Scrambler.

"**Right, time to head back to the cabin,**" said Bob.

He looked around. All of the children were inside the bivouac!

"**Can't we stay here?**" asked Cassia. "**We built it ourselves!**"

"We want Scrambler to stay with us, because he got the badgers to come out!" said Saffron.

"And that makes him the coolest Badger Patrol member ever!" Sunny chimed in.

"Oh, wow!" said Scrambler.
"I wasn't prepared for that!"

Wicked!

Scrambled Up!

Scrambler has been whizzing round Sunflower Valley. Follow each track down from the bushes and write the letter in the muddy puddle to unscramble his name.

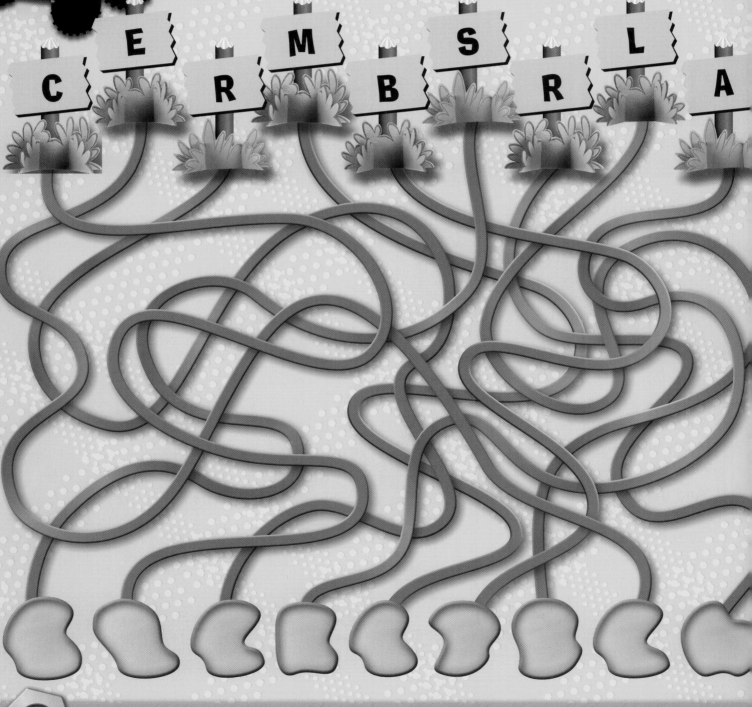

Bob the Builder has a lot of tools to carry. Colour in this picture of him, using the dots to help you get the colours just right.

Two the Same

Find two trucks that are exactly the same.

Answer on page 68.

Truck Counting

How many wheels can you see? How many doors can you see?
How many builders in yellow hats are there?
When you have counted them, point to the right number!

On a building site everyone must wear a hard hat to keep them safe.

1 2 3 4 5 6

Spud the DJ

One day, on their way back from picking sunflowers, Travis, Scruffty and Spud were driving past the radio station.

"Stop!" shouted Spud, excited. **"That's the radio station, where Mike Turntable works!"**

"He's such a good DJ," Travis said.

"Oh, I wish I could be like him!" said Spud. He ran into the radio station.

Stop!

Mike Turntable was sat behind his microphone.

"Hi, I'm the funky DJ, Mike Turntable! How can I help you?"

"Oh, I'm Spud the scarecrow, but I want to be a DJ just like you!"

"Well, Spud, why don't you look after the radio station while I go into Bobsville to collect my new microphone?"

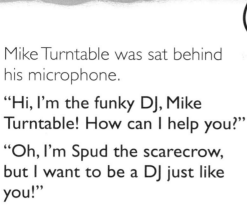

Mike showed Spud which button to press to play the music, and how to speak into the microphone so the listeners could hear him.

"And don't forget," Mike said to Spud, **"when you tell stories on the radio, bigger is better!"**

Spud tried to think of a story to tell. He saw a leaf blow past the window.

"It's a bit windy! I'll tell everyone about that ..."

Over at Bobland Bay, Bob and Wendy were building a new Bob-house. They were listening to the radio while putting up the wall panels.

"We should finish soon, Wendy, if there aren't any delays," said Bob.

Suddenly, a special notice came on the radio.

"High winds will be blowing through Sunflower Valley!" announced Spud the DJ.

"Oh no!" said Wendy. **"We must finish building before the winds get here!"**

Oh no!

Back at the radio station, Spud sat back and chuckled.

"Everyone's going to love my tale about the gales," he said to Scruffty. **"Maybe I'll make the story even bigger!"**

He turned the microphone back on and announced, **"Strong winds will blow through Bobland Bay, any minute now!"**

At the building site, Bob and his team were making everything safe. Mayor Bentley rode up on Scrambler and announced that everyone had to get to safety quickly.

"What about Spud?" asked Wendy. **"He's alone at the radio station!"**

"Don't worry, Scoop and I will rescue him!" said Bob.

Get to safety!

Spud was talking into his microphone when Bob and Scoop arrived.

"Spud, we've come to take you to safety!" said Bob.

"There aren't really any high winds coming, Bob," said Spud. **"That was just an exciting story I made up for my listeners."**

"But Spud, everyone thinks your story is real!"

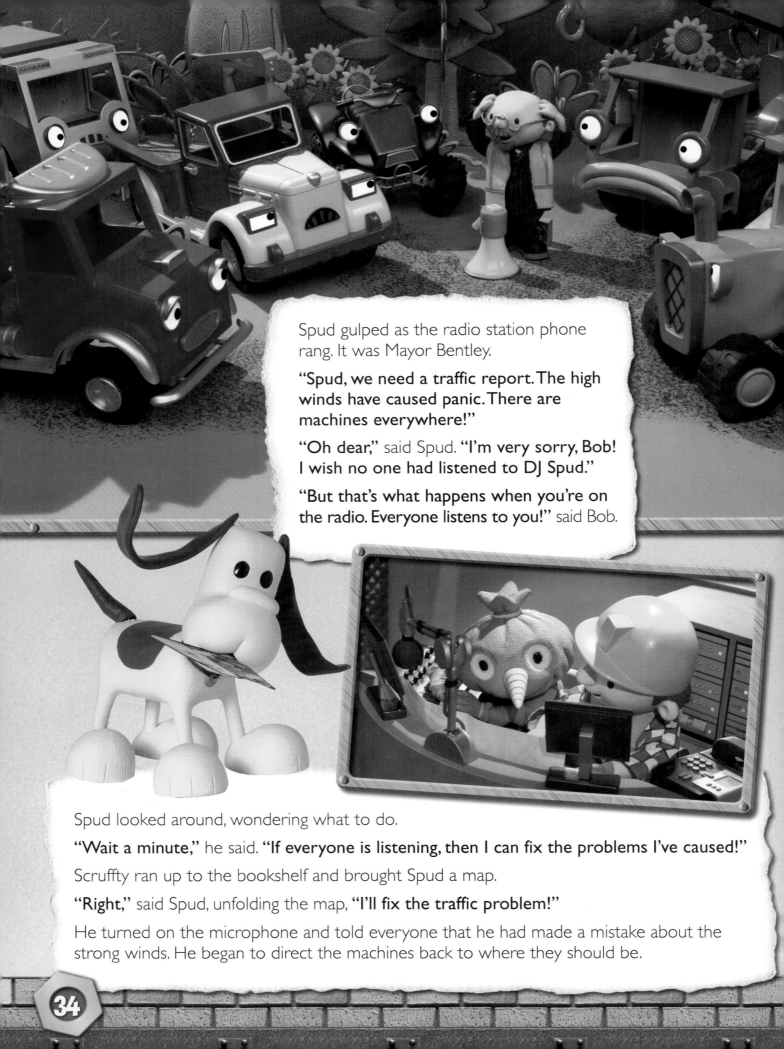

Spud gulped as the radio station phone rang. It was Mayor Bentley.

"Spud, we need a traffic report. The high winds have caused panic. There are machines everywhere!"

"Oh dear," said Spud. "I'm very sorry, Bob! I wish no one had listened to DJ Spud."

"But that's what happens when you're on the radio. Everyone listens to you!" said Bob.

Spud looked around, wondering what to do.

"Wait a minute," he said. "If everyone is listening, then I can fix the problems I've caused!"

Scruffty ran up to the bookshelf and brought Spud a map.

"Right," said Spud, unfolding the map, "I'll fix the traffic problem!"

He turned on the microphone and told everyone that he had made a mistake about the strong winds. He began to direct the machines back to where they should be.

Later that afternoon, Mike Turntable arrived back at the radio station to find Spud slumped in his chair.

"That was very hard work, Mr Turntable," said Spud.
"I think I'll stick to scaring crows!

Thanks Spud!

Back at Bobland Bay, Bob and the team were putting the final touches to the house just as Packer drove up with the new family.

"Here we are," said Packer. "This is Mr Gillis, Mrs Gillis and Billy Gillis."

"Great," said Bob. "I think you're going to like living here!"

"Me too!" said Billy. "We listened to the radio on the way here. Is DJ Spud on every day?"

"Oh no!" said Bob. "That would be far too much trouble to handle!"

Machine Pairs

You will need: 18 pieces of paper, big enough to cover the machines. Somebody to play with!

This is a game for two players. Have a look at the machines on the pages, before covering them up with pieces of paper. Take it in turns to pick up one piece of paper from the left page, and then one piece of paper from the right page where you think the matching machine is. If you're wrong, put the pieces of paper back. The player who matches up the most machines, wins!

Mud Maze

Help this dumper truck find its way out of the deep mud.

The best vehicles for driving through mud are all-terrain, four-wheel drive vehicles like Scrambler. The bigger the tyres, the better for getting through mud. Machines with tracks are also used on very uneven or muddy ground.

Start

Finish

Silent Scoop

"**R**ight team, today we're going to dig and tile the new Bobland Bay Hotel swimming pool," said Bob.

"I love digging!" said Scoop, banging his scoop on the ground.

Bob chuckled. "**Scoop, you and Muck can collect DJ Mike from the radio station and then start digging. Packer, you can come to Bobsville with me, to pick up the tiles.**"

"DJ Mike Turntable?" said Scoop and Muck, wide-eyed.

"Yep," said Bob. "**He will DJ at the pool opening party. He'll need plenty of rest after his night shift on Bob FM.**"

Aloha!

Suddenly, Wendy appeared wearing a grass skirt and shaking maracas.

"Aloha, everyone! The pool party has a Tropical Beach theme. I'm making the decorations!"

"There's a lot to do, so let's dive in!" said Bob.

At the radio station, a tired Mike Turntable was just finishing his radio show.

"This is a personal fave of mine by The Pickers – the perfect song to fall asleep to."

"Hello, Mr Turntable," said Scoop, as Mike left the station. "I'm Scoop and this is Muck. We're here to take you home."

"Call me DJ Mike." He yawned and stretched his arms.

Scoop peeked inside. "Why have you got egg boxes on the wall, DJ Mike?"

"It's soundproofing," said the DJ. "To keep the DJ noise in, and the outside noise out!"

Scoop had an idea. "Why don't you sleep at the hotel, DJ Mike? Then you can get straight out of bed and DJ at the party!"

"Scoop-tastic idea," said DJ Mike. "Let's go!"

Scoop-tastic idea!

Back at the hotel, DJ Mike had gone to sleep in one of the guest villas. Muck and Scoop started work on the pool.

"Can we do it?" yelled Scoop.

"Yes, we can!" Scoop and Muck banged their scoops on the ground.

"Did I just hear thunder?" said a sleepy DJ Mike, sticking his head out of the window. He yawned and went back inside.

"We'll have to dig very quietly!" Muck whispered to Scoop.

Later that afternoon, Muck and Scoop still hadn't dug much. It was hard work trying to be quiet! Muck knocked over a flowerpot and a sleepy DJ Mike looked out of the window again.

"It will take ages to dig the pool quietly," said Scoop. "Bob and Wendy will be here soon with the tiles and decorations!"

The hotel manager Dickie Chester walked up to the pool site. "Where's the pool?" he asked, looking worried.

"Don't worry, Mr Chester, we'll finish it in time," said Scoop.

"If you say so ..." said Dickie, walking off.

Soundproofing!

"There must be a way of digging quickly and quietly," Muck said to Scoop.

"I know!" said Scoop. "Soundproofing! We'll keep the outside noise out of DJ Mike's room!"

Scoop rushed around Sunflower Valley collecting empty boxes and egg cartons. Then he and Muck stuck them all to the outside of the villa. To see if the soundproofing worked, both machines banged about.

"He can't hear us!" said Muck. "Let's get mucky!"

Scoop and Muck were still digging when Dickie walked up and saw the cardboard-covered guest villa.

"That's got to come down!" said Dickie, ignoring Muck and Scoop's protests.

Bob and Packer arrived with the tiles, and Wendy arrived with the decorations.

"Er, where's the pool?" asked Bob. Scoop and Muck explained what was going on. Suddenly, the guest villa shook, and the cardboard fell off as DJ Mike came out.

"Can you keep the noise down?" he said. "I'm trying to sleep!"

Scoop rolled off, sadly, and Bob followed him.

"I thought DJ Mike would have a rest, and that we would dig the pool quickly," said Scoop. "But it's all gone wrong."

"Sometimes you have to think things through, Scoop," said Bob, kindly.

"I wish I could fix it all," said Scoop.

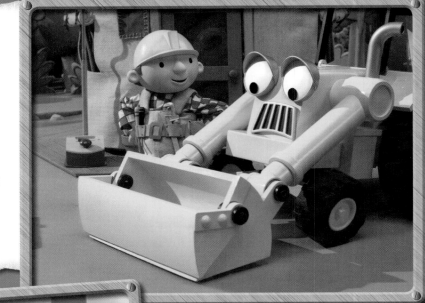

Bob and Scoop wondered what to do. They could hear The Pickers' song DJ Mike had played earlier coming out of Mr Beasley's yurt.

"Hey! That's the song that sends DJ Mike to sleep!" said Scoop, excited. He rushed off to the radio station.

A little while later, The Pickers were ready with their instruments in the radio booth. Scoop announced them to the listeners, and they began to play.

At the hotel, Bob crept into DJ Mike's room and slipped some headphones over his head, so The Pickers' music could keep him asleep.

Now that they could be noisy, Scoop and Muck finished digging the hole. Bob tiled the pool and Wendy put up her decorations. Finally, everything was ready for the opening party.

Mayor Bentley stood at the side of the pool.

"It gives me great pleasure to declare the Bobland Bay Hotel Swimming Pool …" Splash! Mayor Bentley dived into the pool and sat in a rubber ring, **"… open!"**

"Hey, where's DJ Mike?" asked Bob, while everyone cheered and clapped.

"He's still fast asleep!" said Dickie.

"Well, there's only thing for it," said Scoop. **"Take it away, Pickers!"**

The Pickers started playing their music and the pool was officially open!

Follow the Story

Now you've read Silent Scoop, can you remember what happened? Put the pictures in order by writing the letters in the boxes.

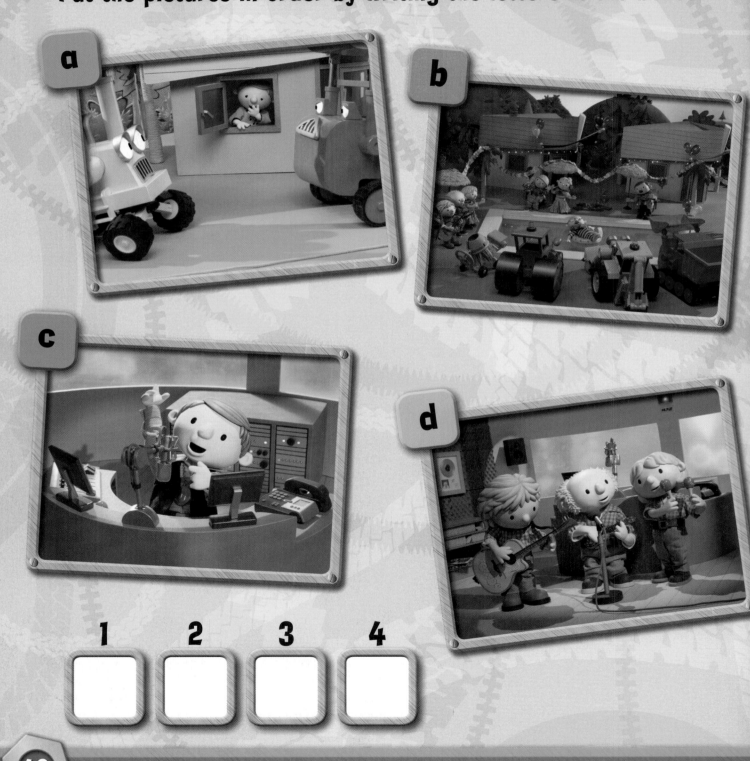

a

b

c

d

1 2 3 4

Answer on page 68.

REAL Machine Remembering

Look at this picture carefully for a few minutes. Then cover it up and see if you can answer these questions.

1) How many REAL machines are there?

2) Is it a sunny or a rainy day?

3) Do the machines have tyres or tracks?

4) What colours are the diggers?

47

Super Splasher

 Bob  Splasher  Travis  Scruffty Ela Isabel

"This is ," told the team. "He's a machine who

can go on land and water! He will give tours of the Valley."

"Splash-erriffic!" cheered . His first tour guest was

, she was looking forward to a relaxing afternoon.

But  hadn't gone far before he spotted the

 tractor in the mud. "I must rescue him!" said ,

"I'm a rescue Superhero!" But  got  mud

everywhere, even over . **SPLAT!** "I didn't need rescuing,"

explained  as he pushed 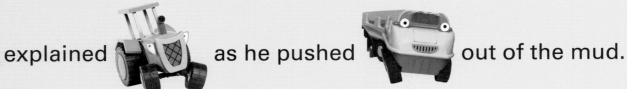 out of the mud.

The next part of the tour was the river ride. As  plunged

into the water he saw  standing on a rock. "He needs

rescuing," cried . As jumped on board he

shook water all over .  SPLASH! drove

back to the shore. "He didn't need rescuing," said Farmer Pickles,

" likes it on that rock." "Oh dear," sighed ,

"I haven't rescued anyone." But just then he saw 's

houseboat drifting down the river. "That houseboat is

floating away.  will save the day!" he cried, speeding

through the  water. But he bumped into the boat and the furniture on the deck fell into the river!  came

to the rescue and pushed all the furniture back to the shore.

"At last, a relaxing afternoon," laughed as she got off

 and rested in one of the chairs!

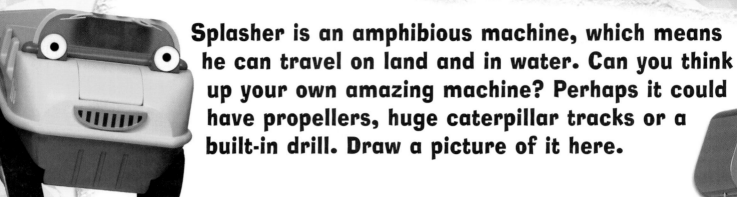

Splasher is an amphibious machine, which means he can travel on land and in water. Can you think up your own amazing machine? Perhaps it could have propellers, huge caterpillar tracks or a built-in drill. Draw a picture of it here.

True or False?

Dizzy is always full of questions. She wants to know if these statements are **TRUE** or **FALSE**. Can you help her? Circle the correct answer.

1) Bob is a train driver. TRUE FALSE

2) Lofty is the tallest of the machines. TRUE FALSE

3) Sumsy is yellow. TRUE FALSE

4) Scruffty is a cat. TRUE FALSE

5) Spud loves to eat cake. TRUE FALSE

6) Flex is a concrete mixer. TRUE FALSE

7) Wendy is an expert at bricklaying. TRUE FALSE

55

Answer on page 68.

REAL Machine Race

The REAL machines are rushing to the building site. Who will get there first? You can play this game with friend. You will need a dice and a counter each. You can use buttons or coins.
Place your counters on the starting square. The first person to roll a 6 starts. Take turns to roll the dice and move your counters. The first counter at the site wins!

FINISH

START

You need more oil, go back 1 space.

The lights are green, move forward 2 spaces.

You get stuck in the mud, go back 2 spaces.

You are driving at high speed, move forward 2 spaces.

You find a shortcut, move forward 2 spaces.

You hit a bump in the road, go back to START.

The lights are red, go back 1 space.

You have a puncture, go back 1 space.

There is a hole in the road, go back 1 space.

Zoomer's Snowy Adventure

One snowy morning, Zoomer was racing down the hills of Sunflower Valley, on his way to Bob's Yard. He passed a goat, a bird and a rabbit – they were all freezing cold with nowhere warm to go and nothing to eat.

"Oh dear!" said Zoomer. "Lots of snow isn't fun for everyone. I'll come back to help after I've finished Bob's important job."

Over at the yard, Bob was speaking to Mr Sabatini.

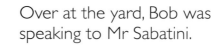

"Don't worry, Mr Sabatini, we'll soon clear the roads and then you can deliver your bread to the General Store!"

Bob put the phone down and turned to look at the igloo the machines had built in the middle of the yard.

"Wow, that's amazing!" said Zoomer, skidding to a halt next to Scoop.

"It's fantastic!" agreed Bob. "You're just in time, Zoomer. I need you to help Scoop clear the road with his snow-plough. He needs to follow your tracks."

"Snow prob, Bob!" said Zoomer proudly.

Bob chuckled. "**Keep to the road, Zoomer, or Scoop will get stuck in the deep snow by the side!**"

Zoomer and Scoop sped off to start clearing the roads, while Bob and Muck headed over to Mr Sabatini's bakery.

"**The track to the General Store is completely blocked!**" said Mr Sabatini.

"Don't worry," said Bob. "We're clearing that road first so you can get your bread to the store."

"I-a don't-a know what we'd-a-do without you and the gang, Bob!" said Mr Sabatini.

Thank you, Bob!

Suddenly Carlo and Cassia ran up, shouting, "Come and see the ducks!"

They all rushed to the frozen pond. The ducks had nothing to eat and nowhere to swim.

"They look so cold and hungry," said Muck, sadly.

"The winter can be very hard for wildlife," said Bob, "especially when it snows."

Carlo and Cassia took bread from their dad to feed the ducks.

"That should-a warm-a them up-a!" he said.

While Bob and Muck began to clear the road to the General Store, Zoomer and Scoop were working at top speed.

"Keep up, Scoop!" yelled Zoomer.

"I'm trying!" laughed Scoop. "But it isn't easy when you don't have snow tracks!"

Zoomer sped off, leaving Scoop to follow his tracks. Suddenly, he saw a rabbit digging in the snow, trying to find his burrow.

"Do you need help finding your home?" Zoomer asked the rabbit. The rabbit nodded and twitched his whiskers. Zoomer rolled up a snow bank to help the rabbit.

"Zoomer!" called Scoop. **"Shall I still follow your tracks?"**

There was no answer so Scoop decided to carry on. He couldn't see any other tracks.

Help!

"Woah!" panicked Scoop. **"It's a bit deep! Zoomer, help!"** Scoop was stuck in deep snow at the side of the road.

Zoomer raced back when he heard Scoop's cries for help. **"Oh no, Scoop, you followed my tracks!"**

"That was the plan!" said Scoop. **"You were supposed to guide me."**

Zoomer explained that he had been searching for the rabbit's burrow.

"Don't worry Scoop, I'll go and find help!" he said.

Muck and Bob had almost finished clearing the road to the General Store when Zoomer raced up.

"Help! I've guided Scoop into a snow bank," said Zoomer. "I'm sorry, Bob."

"Show us where Scoop is so we can rescue him," said Bob.

Zoomer led the way back to where Scoop was stuck. When they arrived, Bob tied one end of a rope to Scoop's rear digger, and the other end to Muck's front digger.

"OK, Muck," said Bob. "Heave away!"

Muck pulled hard and Scoop came rolling out of the snow.

"So why did you go off the track?" Bob asked Zoomer.

Zoomer told Bob about the lost rabbit.

"The snow has caused lots of problems," said Bob, thoughtfully. "But I've got an idea that just might work!"

Bob and Muck rushed back to the yard, leaving Scoop and Zoomer to finish clearing the track.

By the evening, the roads were finally clear and Mr Sabatini's bread had reached the general store. As the tired machines arrived back at the yard, Bob was smiling.

"Look over there, Zoomer!" he said.

"Wow!" said Zoomer as he saw Wendy laying out breadcrumbs at the door of the igloo the machines had built earlier.

"I thought the igloo would make the perfect animal shelter!" said Bob.

"Thanks Bob, it's brilliant!" said Zoomer. **"Now the animals have somewhere warm to sleep!"**

Snowy Search

Can you find these different ways of getting around in the snow hidden in the word square? Words can read across and down.

ski   snowmobile
sled   snowplough
skate   snowshoes
             snowboard

s	n	o	w	m	o	b	i	l	e
n	s	a	d	h	k	p	t	s	c
o	n	s	k	i	f	l	m	p	r
w	o	r	a	c	g	j	y	a	d
p	w	o	e	s	l	e	d	q	v
l	s	i	m	t	w	z	g	o	e
o	h	p	s	k	a	t	e	c	a
u	o	z	o	o	m	e	r	d	t
g	e	h	j	t	l	d	r	a	o
h	s	n	o	w	b	o	a	r	d

There is one word in the square that isn't in the list. Here's a clue to help you find it:

He zooms around the snowy hills of Sunflower Valley!

The missing word is:

___ ___ ___ ___ ___ ___ ___ ___

Answer on page 68.

Crane Spotting

These pictures look the same but 5 things are different in picture 2. Can you spot them all?

1

TM 1050-3.1

2

TM 1050-3.1

6465

This mobile crane is on its way to the site. The hook is attached to the front of the cab to stop it swinging around as it moves along.

65

Answers on page 68.

REAL Machine Quiz

Find out if you are a REAL machine expert now, with Wendy's questions. Look back through the book to answer the questions, then use the secret code to turn your number answers into letters.

The letters will complete the special message from Bob and the team. **Good luck!**

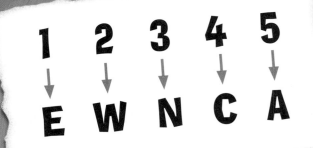

1	2	3	4	5
↓	↓	↓	↓	↓
E	W	N	C	A

1

On page 47, how many white cabs can you see?

. . . .

2

On page 39, how many dumper trucks are stuck in the mud?

. . . .

3 On page 10, how many wheels does the concrete truck mixer have on each side? . . . .

4 On page 28, how many yellow trucks are there? . . . .

5 On page 29, which number is coloured green? . . . .

"Can we fix it? Yes, _ _   _ _ _ _ !"

Answers

Page 18 Picture C is missing the basket.

Page 28 Trucks b and f are exactly the same.

Page 29 You can see 1 wheel, 4 doors and 6 builders.

Page 38

Page 46 c=1, a=2, d=3, b=4.

Page 55 1) FALSE 2) TRUE 3) FALSE 4) FALSE
5) TRUE 6) FALSE 7) TRUE

Page 64 The missing word is "Zoomer". >>>>>

Page 65 1) The warning stripes are green.
2) The cab has a number on the front.
3) A front wheel is missing.
4) The sky has more clouds.
5) The side window is missing.

Pages 66-67 1)2, 2)1, 3)4, 4)5, 6)3 – "Can we fix it? Yes, WE CAN!"

Advertisement
JOIN BOB'S BUSY TEAM WITH
Bob the Builder™
MAGAZINE
CBeebies BBC
on sale EVERY 3 WEEKS
FANTASTIC FREE GIFTS!
STICKERS
FUN with REAL MACHINES!
FUN Workbook INSIDE!
STORIES PLUS ACTIVITIES!
POINT TO YOUR FAVOURITE MACHINE